A FOX
GOT MY SOCKS

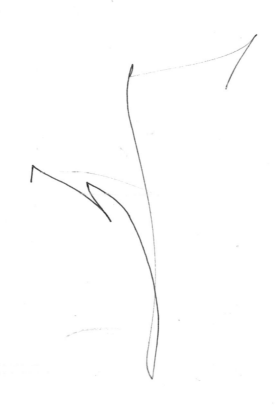

For Charlie Everton Bingham

A Red Fox Book

Published by Random House Children's Books
20 Vauxhall Bridge Road, London SW1V 2SA

A division of Random House UK Ltd
London Melbourne Sydney Auckland
Johannesburg and agencies throughout the world

© Hilda Offen 1992

3 5 7 9 10 8 6 4 2

First published in 1992 by Hutchinson Children's Books

Red Fox edition 1994
This edition 1996

Designed by Paul Welti

Printed in Singapore

RANDOM HOUSE UK Limited Reg. No. 954009

ISBN 0 09 971821 9

A FOX
GOT MY SOCKS
Hilda Offen

RED FOX

Yesterday
was washing day.

Pretend to wash

My clothes flip-flapped
and blew away.

Flap arms

A cat got my hat.

Touch head with both hands

A fox got my socks.

Touch both feet

A goat got my coat.

Pretend to do up buttons

An owl got my towel.

Pretend to flap towel

'Oh no!' said the pig.
'These pants are too big!'

Pretend to hold up pants

And the bear gave a snort:
'This jumper's too short!'

Pull jumper up

Two baby llamas
were in my pyjamas

Touch chest and knee

And where was my scarf?
Wrapped round a giraffe!

Pretend to wrap scarf

But the sun was so hot,

Fan face

I said, 'Keep what you've got.

Hold out arms

I'm perfectly happy ...

... to stay in my nappy!'

Dance around

Some
bestselling Red Fox
picture books